Unlocking the Secrets of Science

Profiling 20th Century Achievers in Science, Medicine, and Technology

Sally Ride: The Story of the First American Female in Space

Linda R. Wade

PO Box 619 • Bear, Delaware 19701
www.mitchelllane.com

Unlocking the Secrets of Science

Profiling 20th Century Achievers in Science, Medicine, and Technology

Marc Andreessen and the Development of the Web Browser
Frederick Banting and the Discovery of Insulin
Jonas Salk and the Polio Vaccine
Wallace Carothers and the Story of DuPont Nylon
Tim Berners-Lee and the Development of the World Wide Web
Robert A. Weinberg and the Search for the Cause of Cancer
Alexander Fleming and the Story of Penicillin
Robert Goddard and the Liquid Rocket Engine
Oswald Avery and the Story of DNA
Edward Teller and the Development of the Hydrogen Bomb
Stephen Wozniak and the Story of Apple Computer
Barbara McClintock: Pioneering Geneticist
Wilhelm Roentgen and the Discovery of X Rays
Gerhard Domagk and the Discovery of Sulfa
Willem Kolff and the Invention of the Dialysis Machine
Robert Jarvik and the First Artificial Heart
Chester Carlson and the Development of Xerography
Joseph E. Murray and the Story of the First Human Kidney Transplant
Albert Einstein and the Theory of Relativity
Edward Roberts and the Story of the Personal Computer
Godfrey Hounsfield and the Invention of CAT Scans
Christiaan Barnard and the Story of the First Successful Heart Transplant
Selman Waksman and the Discovery of Streptomycin
Paul Ehrlich and Modern Drug Development
Sally Ride: The Story of the First American Female in Space
Luis Alvarez and the Development of the Bubble Chamber
Jacques-Yves Cousteau: His Story Under the Sea
Francis Crick and James Watson: Pioneers in DNA Research
Raymond Damadian and the Development of the MRI
William Hewlett: Pioneer of the Computer Age
Linus Pauling and the Chemical Bond
Willem Einthoven and the Story of Electrocardiography
Edwin Hubble and the Theory of the Expanding Universe
Henry Ford and the Assembly Line
Enrico Fermi and the Nuclear Reactor
Otto Hahn and the Story of Nuclear Fission
Charles Richter and the Story of the Richter Scale
Philo T. Farnsworth: The Life of Television's Forgotten Inventor
John R. Pierce: Pioneer in Satellite Communications

Sally Ride: The Story of the First American Female in Space

Printing   1   2   3   4   5   6   7   8   9   10

Library of Congress Cataloging-in-Publication Data
Wade, Linda R.
    Sally Ride: the story of the first American female in space/Linda Wade.
       p. cm. — (Unlocking the secrets of science)
    Summary: A biography of Sally Ride, who in 1983 became the first American woman to travel in space.
    Includes bibliographical references and index.
    ISBN 1-58415-139-0 (lib. bdg.)
    1. Ride, Sally—Juvenile literature. 2. Astronauts—United States—Biography—Juvenile literature. 3. Women astronauts—United States—Biography—Juvenile literature. [1. Ride, Sally. 2. Astronauts. 3. Women—Biography.] I. Title. II. Series.
TL789.85.R53 W33 2002
629.45'0092—dc21
[B]   2002066128

ABOUT THE AUTHOR: Linda R. Wade is a retired school librarian. She served 23 years in the same school she attended as a child. She has taught writing, both locally and nationally at writing conferences. She received her education from Olivet Nazarene University and Indiana University. She has published 30 books since 1989. She and her husband, Edward, like to travel across the United States visiting their children, historic places, and national parks.

SPECIAL THANKS: from the author to Carole Zilz of the Allen County Public Library. She was my right hand while I was writing this book.
PHOTO CREDITS: All photographs are courtesy of NASA.

PUBLISHER'S NOTE: In selecting those persons to be profiled in this series, we first attempted to identify the most notable accomplishments of the 20th century in science, medicine, and technology. When we were done, we noted a serious deficiency in the inclusion of women. For the greater part of the 20th century science, medicine, and technology were male-dominated fields. In many cases, the contributions of women went unrecognized. Women have tried for years to be included in these areas, and in many cases, women worked side by side with men who took credit for their ideas and discoveries. Even as we move forward into the 21st century, we find women still sadly underrepresented. It is not an oversight, therefore, that we profiled mostly male achievers. Information simply does not exist to include a fair selection of women.

Contents

In June 1983, Sally Ride became America's first female in space. She paved the way for future women astronauts.

Chapter 1

A Day That Made History

• •

On June 18, 1983, five astronauts lay on their backs in the *Challenger* spacecraft at Kennedy Space Center at Cape Canaveral, Florida. Four of them were men; the fifth was Sally Ride. She would become America's first woman in space. She was indeed a pioneer.

At launch minus seven minutes the walkway was pulled away. The power units started whirring and sent a shudder through the shuttle. The astronauts closed the visors on their helmets and began to breathe from the oxygen supply.

At 31 seconds before liftoff, the shuttle's onboard computers took charge. Then came the count. *Ten, nine, eight, seven*—the orbiter's three main engines began to burn fuel from the huge orange tank—*six, five, four, three, two, one.* The rockets lit. There was no turning back. The long-awaited moment had arrived.

Sally Ride didn't hear the words *We have liftoff.* All she heard was rumbling. Outside, large white clouds of smoke covered the launch platform. The roar was deafening. And then the Space Transport System began to lift off the launchpad.

Faster and faster it went. In 30 seconds it was already a mile from the launch site. Two minutes after launch the twin boosters, empty, broke away and began a parachute glide to Earth. Then suddenly the ride became smooth and quiet.

Left to right on the flight deck: Norman Thagard, Robert Crippen, Frederick Hauck, Sally Ride, and John Fabian. A pre-set 35mm camera exposed this picture on board the Space Shuttle Challenger, 6/83.

Six minutes after launch the big orange tank was also empty and it fell away. It would reenter Earth's atmosphere and break into tiny pieces.

Sally described how she felt at that point. "The force pushing us against the back of our seats steadily increases. We can barely move because we're being held in place by a force of 3 g's—three times the force of gravity we feel on Earth. At first we don't mind it—we've all felt much more than that when we've done aerobatics in our jet training airplanes. But that lasted only a few seconds and this seemed to go on forever. After a couple of minutes of 3 g's, we're uncomfortable, straining to hold our books on our laps and craning our necks against the force to read the instruments. I find myself wishing we'd hurry up and get into orbit."

At launch plus eight and one half minutes the engines cut off and the force was gone—even the normal one g she was used to feeling on Earth.

Sally Ride was taking the ride of her life. She was in space. She was making history. In a few minutes the shuttle would get another boost to send it into orbit. She would fly 160 miles above the Earth and experience a sunrise and sunset every 90 minutes for 6 days, 2 hours and 24 minutes. During that time, Sally and the crew of the Space Shuttle *Challenger* would launch two commercial satellites and retrieve a West German Shuttle Pallet Satellite (SPAS 01).

This was the adventure of a lifetime, not only for Sally Ride, but also for the United States.

In 1961, John F. Kennedy became President of the United States. Five months after he took the oath of office, he announced to Congress that the nation should make a commitment to landing a man on the moon and bringing him safely back to Earth. Sally Ride was in her teens when Kennedy was President and his speech made her think about the possibilities.

Chapter 2

From Classroom to Tennis Court to Astrophysics

• •

Sally Kristen Ride was born on May 26, 1951, in Encino, California (near Los Angeles). Two years later her sister, Karen, was born. Sally called Karen "Bear" because it was easier to say when she was a little girl.

Dale and Joyce Ride were the girls' parents. Dale Ride taught political science at Santa Monica College. Joyce was also a teacher, but while the girls were young, she chose to stay at home with them. She did some volunteer work at the Encino Presbyterian Church and was a counselor at a nearby prison for women. She also taught English to foreign students.

Neither parent pushed Sally or her sister in any particular direction. They wanted the girls to explore and follow a path in life made for them. About the only pressure the Rides put on the girls was to study hard and do their best.

Sally was an early reader. She especially enjoyed reading the sports section of the newspaper. Each Sunday morning she'd race out to get the paper. Then she'd find a cozy chair and curl up with it. She memorized the players and their statistics. She also liked to read mysteries and science fiction. If the story had a lot of action, Sally wanted to read it. Superman was her biggest hero.

Not only did Sally read about sports, she joined in the games. She loved to play soccer, baseball and football with the neighborhood children. However, softball was her favorite game. Sometimes she was the only girl, but when the sides were picked, she was always one of the first to be chosen.

As a political science professor, Dale Ride met people from many different countries. He often invited foreign students and visitors from the various cultures to come over for dinner. Sally and Bear loved to hear their stories. They learned about the customs, languages, and religions of other lands. These visits helped to broaden their education.

The family enjoyed traveling together. When Sally was only nine years old, Dale and Joyce decided to tour Europe for a year. Dale took a leave of absence from the Santa Monica College. He and Joyce tutored Sally and Bear and took them to many wonderful places. The girls would tour a castle one day and explore mountains and valleys the next. They learned about the different governments and how life varied in the European cities. They remembered the stories told by visitors who had come to their home. In 1983, Joyce told the *Chicago Tribune,* "They learned as much traveling as they would have in school."

In fact, when Sally returned to the classroom, she was far ahead of her classmates. The school moved her up a grade. The trip to Europe had broadened the girls' education far more than expected.

Dale and Joyce began playing tennis. Sally thought the game looked interesting, so they bought a racket for her. This was a new challenge, and Sally loved challenges. Soon she was out on the driveway banging a tennis ball against the garage door. Hour after hour she practiced. She got so she could aim at a spot and hit it with the tennis ball.

On the court she was a villain. All this practice led her to challenge everyone who played the game. She lived to play tennis, and she didn't care if her opponent was someone her age or an adult.

By the time she was 11 she was training with Alice Marble. Marble was a four-time national women's tennis champion, and she was a great teacher. Sally was soon playing on the national junior tennis circuit. She spent her weekends competing in tennis tournaments across the country.

It wasn't long before she ranked nationally as an amateur. Because of this ranking she received a scholarship to Westlake School for Girls. Westlake is a small private high school in Los Angeles.

Sally was a good student in school, especially if the subject grabbed her interest. When she was a junior she took a physiology class, about how living things work. This class captivated her. It was the academic challenge she had been looking for.

The teacher was Dr. Elizabeth Mommaerts. She loved science and soon saw the interest that Sally had in the subject. Sally thought Dr. Mommaerts was an intelligent, clear-thinking, and independent-minded person. Dr. Mommaerts taught Sally to love science by giving her special experiments to do. She showed her interesting science books to read and told Sally how important math is to a scientist.

Sally learned about the scientific method and how scientists use this method to solve problems. Dr. Mommaerts told the class about the steps that scientists use to process information. Those steps include observation, hypothesizing, gathering data, organizing data, and drawing conclusions. She showed the class how scientists use this method of experimentation, along with careful measurements and analysis of data, to gain a better understanding of the universe.

This class changed Sally's life. Science was exciting! Solving problems was exciting! School became even more wonderful to her, and Dr. Mommaerts replaced Superman as Sally's role model.

Sally could not hide her enthusiasm. She wanted to learn more. Dr. Mommaerts encouraged Sally to pursue a career in science. With her encouragement and that of both her parents, Sally knew she could do anything she wanted to do.

This was in the 1960s, when Sally was in her teens. Her interest in science led to an interest in the stars and space travel. She wondered what it would be like to travel in space. Those were the days when the United States was competing with the USSR in a race to get into space.

President John F. Kennedy made an important speech to Congress on May 25, 1961. "I believe that this Nation should commit itself to achieving the goal, before this decade is out, of landing a man on the moon and returning him safely to earth. No single space project in this period will be more impressive to mankind, or more important for the long-range exploration of space; and none will be so difficult or expensive to accomplish. . . . But in a very real sense, it will not be one man going to the moon—if we make this judgment affirmatively, it will be an entire nation. For all of us must work to put him there."

Sally listened and thought about the possibilities. She would look at the night sky and imagine being up there among the stars.

Then the word came that all Americans waited for. The Ride family joined millions of people as they held their breath and watched Alan Shepard ride the *Freedom 7* into space on May 5, 1961. That 15-minute flight made all America cheer.

They worried when Virgil Grissom's *Liberty Bell 7* sank on July 21, 1961, following its landing in the Atlantic Ocean. And they cheered when the nearby helicopter rescued Grissom from the water.

A U.S. Marines helicopter hovers over the Liberty Bell 7 as it tries to rescue Virgil Grissom on July 21, 1961. The Mercury-Redstone 4 test flight was launched from Cape Canaveral. The spacecraft sank and was lost in the ocean during the post landing recovery period. Grissom was picked up by the helicopter and brought to safety.

They continued to watch as various astronauts went up in the Mercury-Atlas spacecrafts. John Glenn became the first American to circle Earth on February 20, 1962. He made three orbits before returning, and Sally cheered his accomplishment.

Then on May 15–16, 1963, Gordon Cooper stayed in space in the Mercury spacecraft *Faith 7* to make 22 orbits of Earth in 34 hours and 20 minutes. Next came the Gemini flights, when two men at a time were sent up in space.

Meanwhile, the Russians were also making headlines. One April 12, 1961, Yuri Gagarin, in *Vostok 1*, became the first person to orbit Earth. By June 1963, five other piloted Vostok spacecraft had also orbited Earth, including *Vostok 6*, piloted by Valentina V. Tereskova, the first woman in space. On October 12, 1964, the USSR sent up the first three-man spacecraft.

The U.S. space program was blossoming. Newspapers across the country carried news of any planned launch date. Television networks sent reporters and photographers to catch all the news. Sally watched and listened with great interest.

In 1968 Sally graduated as one of the top six students from Westlake School for Girls. She was soon off to Swarthmore College in Swarthmore, Pennsylvania, with plans to become a scientist. She didn't think she would ever be an astronaut, but she knew she wanted to learn everything she could about space. She majored in physics and continued playing tennis. She played in the Eastern Intercollegiate Women's Tennis championship and won two years in a row.

When winter came, Sally found it difficult to get good practice time. It was cold in Pennsylvania, and snow often covered the tennis courts. She missed the warm California weather. She finally decided to leave Swarthmore and transferred to Stanford University in Palo Alto, California.

The original seven Mercury astronauts—From left, first row: Walter Schirra, Jr., Donald Slayton, John Glenn, Scott Carpenter. Back: Alan Shepard, Jr., Vrigil Grissom, and Gordon Cooper.

Her days at Stanford were full of math and science classes. She enrolled in astronomy and loved it. Astrophysics was another class that dealt with the science of stars and other objects in space, and Sally found herself totally fascinated with the subject.

Sally decided to take some English literature classes. She especially enjoyed Shakespeare. His works were not easy to understand, so she approached them as problems to be solved. She made a game of finding the clues he hid in his plays and then tried to figure out the ending.

During all these years, the space program continued. Neil A. Armstrong and Edwin E. Aldrin, Jr. rode the *Apollo 11* spacecraft to the moon. Armstrong left the module and explored the moon's surface on July 20, 1969. The words Armstrong said when he touched the moon that day rang in the nation's ears. "That's one small step for man, one giant leap for mankind."

Sally continued to watch these flights, but there were no American women astronauts. Then, the National Aeronautics and Space Administration (NASA) started recruiting scientists as well as jet pilots to go into space.

To stay in good physical condition, Sally ran five miles a day. She played intramural sports, including rugby. This roughneck game is similar to football.

In 1972 a famous tennis player named Billie Jean King watched Sally in a tennis match. King suggested that Sally quit school and become a professional tennis player, but Sally refused. She wanted to be a space scientist, and nothing was more important to her than that, not even the sport she loved so much.

Sally graduated from Stanford University in 1973 with a bachelor of science degree in physics and a bachelor of arts degree in English. This was unusual because both degrees are so difficult to earn.

She continued on at Stanford and earned a master of science degree in physics in 1975. She decided to stay at school and work for her Ph.D.

Her graduate work included research in X-ray astronomy and free-electron lasers. She wondered about the X rays given off by distant stars. For her doctoral dissertation, she investigated the theoretical behavior of free electrons in a magnetic field. This was a phenomenon she studied almost entirely in the abstract, as sets of equations.

Sally enjoyed graduate school. She helped the professors do research and enjoyed searching for answers. She also helped them in the classroom. These two activities are often part of a graduate student's day, but for Sally, they were her day. She loved her work. Little did she know that the work she was doing as a graduate student would be relevant to the long-range NASA project of studying ways to transmit power from orbiting space stations to Earth.

During her final year of graduate work, Sally knew it was time to make some real career decisions. She was completing her ninth year of college. She had a lot of education and experience in the lab as well as in the classroom, but how would she use all this knowledge?

She began to explore her possibilities. She looked for research jobs in her field. Then she read the college newspaper advertisements. It was there that she found the notice that changed her life.

Left to right: The crew of STS-7— Dr. Norman Thagard and Sally Ride, both mission specialists, Commander Robert Crippen, John Fabian, mission specialist, and Pilot Frederick Hauck participate in a press conference near the termination point of the emergency slide wire system at the Complex 39A launch site. The astronauts were at the launch site in preparation for the seventh mission of the Space Shuttle.

Chapter 3

A Life-Changing Advertisement

● ●

When Sally Ride picked up the college newspaper, she found an intriguing announcement: NASA was looking for a new group of astronauts. With the larger space shuttle that NASA was using, more astronauts could travel into space. These new astronauts would be called mission specialists and would conduct experiments in space. NASA needed engineers, scientists and physicians.

Sally later wrote, "Suddenly I knew that I wanted a chance to see the Earth and the stars from outer space." She applied to be an astronaut the very day she saw the notice.

Sally was not the only one to see the advertisement. More than eight thousand other people responded to the ad. Over one thousand of these responses were from women. NASA sorted through all these applications and narrowed the field to 208 finalists. Sally made the cut.

The finalists were divided into small groups and asked to come to Johnson Space Center in Houston, Texas. Sally had to answer many questions and take many tests, including physical tests and mental stress tests. In one test, Sally was put into a small round compartment made of fabric. It was called the crystal rescue sphere. There was room for only one person. This compartment was designed to transport a crew member from one space vehicle to another in case there were not enough pressurized space suits for everyone.

Each astronaut took stress tests to see how he or she reacted to stressful situations. This was important because the life of an astronaut demands long, hard hours of tedious mental and physical work. NASA wanted people who were fine scientists, who knew how to be team players, who could work with other people to get a job done. It wanted astronauts who could stay calm and make good decisions, even when things were not going just right.

Each applicant was interviewed by several people and given a medical examination. Sally listened to talks about what it was like to be an astronaut. Then she was interviewed by two different psychiatrists and by a 10-member selection committee. At the end of a week, she went home to finish the last two months of school.

Sally received her Ph.D. in 1978 from Stanford University. She was on the brink of a new career, one that even she could not have imagined.

On January 16, 1978, Sally received a call from George Abbey, director of flight operations at Johnson Space Center. "We've got a job here for you, if you're still interested in taking it," he said.

"Yes sir," Sally answered.

Out of over eight thousand applicants, Sally Ride was one of 35 people chosen for the astronaut training class of 1978. They called themselves the "Thirty-Five New Guys" (TFNG), even though six of them were women. Training for the TFNGs began at Johnson Space Center in July. For one year, they were officially called astronaut candidates (ASCANs).

Sally was a student again. She studied computer science and engineering. She learned how each part of the space shuttle worked. She even learned how to fly a T-38 training jet. For about 15 hours a week she sat in the backseat of the jet and learned about radio communications and navigation. She experienced the higher levels of g forces. The plane had two sets of controls, one in front and one in back. The pilots sometimes let Sally fly the plane using the controls in back. She liked flying so much that in her free time she took lessons to get her private pilot's license.

During that first year of training, as part of a survival course, Sally learned parachute jumping and the techniques of water survival. This was the most physically demanding part of the training. She was dropped into rough water from a helicopter at four hundred feet and left floating on a small raft. Another time she was shoved out of a motorboat while wearing an open parachute. She had to get out of the parachute harness while being dragged through the water by the boat.

Sally was glad for all the hours of running and strength training. Because she was so strong, she was able to get through the survival part of her astronaut training.

At the space center there was a machine called a simulator. Sitting in front of the simulator made Sally feel like she was riding in a real rocket. She enjoyed this part of her training. She said it made her feel like she was riding a roller coaster.

She spent 12 to 15 hours a week in the shuttle simulator in Houston. She describes her simulator training this way: "They turn you on your back and shake you and vibrate you and pump noise in, so that it's very realistic."

Sally Ride officially became an astronaut in 1979. Now she could be assigned to a spaceflight. She became part of an engineering team that worked with a Canadian manufacturer to design a remote manipulator system (RMS).

The RMS was a 50-foot-long robotic arm used to move payloads, or cargo, in and out of the shuttle's cargo bay. It was not easy to use. Sally spent two years learning how to operate the arm. She helped work out corrective procedures in case of a breakdown. John Fabian also worked on the RMS. He and Sally became experts; their knowledge would be very important because of the projects scheduled for future spaceflights.

As part of her training, Sally also learned how to be a capsule communicator, or capcom. The capcom is the only person who has direct communication with both the flight crew during a mission and Mission Control. Capcoms must understand everything about the mission. They have to stay calm, even during emergencies, to relay messages between Mission Control and the crew aboard the shuttle. Sally was the first woman given this responsibility. She sat in that important seat during the second and third shuttle flights.

Sally Ride was certainly proving her ability to be on a space mission. She understood the many jobs on a mission into space. She had done well as a capcom.

In April 1982, Navy Captain Robert L. Crippen, the commander of the seventh scheduled shuttle mission, on which the robot arm was to be tested in space for the first time, personally chose Sally Ride for his crew. In addition to serving as mission specialist, Ride was to act as flight engineer, assisting the commander and the shuttle pilot during ascent, reentry, and landing.

NASA announced the entire crew. They were Robert Crippen, commander; Frederick "Rick" Hauck, copilot; and mission specialists John Fabian and Sally Ride. Norman Thagard became the fifth crew member in December of that year. As a physician, his job was to investigate a nagging difficulty of space travel: the initial queasiness, or "space adaptation syndrome," that seemed to afflict about 50 percent of all astronauts during their first few days of weightlessness.

Newspaper and magazine reporters wanted to interview Sally. She did not like all the attention. She told *Newsweek* reporter Pamela Abramson, "I did not come to NASA to make history. It's important to me that people don't think I was picked for the flight because I am a woman and it's time for NASA to send one."

In July, amid all the preparations for her spaceflight, Sally married Steven Hawley. Steven was a fellow astronaut and astronomer and would fly on the twelfth *Challenger* mission. Sally flew herself to the wedding, which was in Salina, Kansas, at the home of Steven's parents. She and Steven lived in a spacious three-bedroom home in Clear Lake City, Texas, near Johnson Space Center.

After the wedding, Sally spent long hours studying the flight manual. It had step-by-step procedures for every part of the flight. She also spent many hours in a simulator, practicing each step over and over again.

Sally Ride was ready to go. She was ready to become the first American woman in space.

The seventh launch of the Space Shuttle and the second lift-off of the Orbiter Challenger occurred at 7:33 am EDT on June 18, 1983. This was Sally Ride's first space flight.

Chapter 4

Up, Up and Away

• •

T he alarm clock was the first thing Sally heard on the morning of June 18, 1983. It was 3:15 and still very dark outside. It was time to get ready.

At the space center, the astronauts dressed in their identical blue flight suits with a large round patch on the right side. Then they had breakfast.

When the sun came up a large crowd was already watching. They could make out the tall white booster rocket standing upright in the distance. The space shuttle *Challenger* was beside the booster.

At three hours before launch, a small van took the crew to launchpad 39-A. The huge digital clock that had begun the countdown two days before was still clicking off the minutes and seconds to liftoff.

The crew looked up at the lighted 30-story-high space shuttle. Sputtering and hissing filled the air. The crew took the elevator up 195 feet to the space shuttle's hatch. Six technicians waited in the white room to help them with their final preparations.

One by one the astronauts put on their helmets and climbed through the hatch. First to enter were Bob Crippen and pilot Rick Hauck. Then Sally Ride and John Fabian took their places behind the first two. Norm Thagard entered last. He rode below the others in the mid-deck section of the orbiter. The technicians strapped the astronauts into their seats, wished them a happy trip, then left the crew alone for the final hour.

It was a busy hour, too. Each astronaut had a special job to do, and each had been chosen because of his or her specialty. Once again they checked their procedure manuals. They double-checked to make sure they were strapped in properly and that the oxygen flow was correct.

Steven radioed his wife from the Shuttle Launch Control. "Sally, have a ball!" he called.

Then it was launch minus seven minutes. The walkway with the white room pulled away.

In her book *To Space & Back,* Sally describes liftoff:

"3 . . . 2 . . . 1 . . . The rockets light! The shuttle leaps off the launchpad in a cloud of steam and trail of fire. Inside, the ride is rough and loud. Our heads are rattling around inside our helmets. We can barely hear the voices from Mission Control in our headsets above the thunder of the rockets and engines. For an instant I wonder if everything is working right. But there's no more time to wonder, and no time to be scared."

Up, up, up the rocket climbed past the clouds. The boosters burned out and fell away like they were supposed to do. The big orange tank was taking them out of Earth's atmosphere. Up there, the sky was black.

The g forces were terrific. For several minutes they could hardly move. Then suddenly the force was gone. The orange tank was empty and fell to Earth. Then a very strange thing happened. Books and pencils began to float in midair. Sally knew that they were finally in space.

Sally's parents were in the crowd of about 250,000 people on the beaches of Cape Canaveral. Also among the crowd were well-known women who had come to watch because Sally Ride was on board. Margaret Heckler and Elizabeth Dole were U.S. government officials. Jane Fonda, Gloria Steinem and other people who were working for women's rights also came to witness the historic flight. For them, Sally showed the progress women were making in performing jobs that before had been done only by men.

At 7:33 A.M. on Saturday, June 18, 1983, people everywhere cheered as Sally Ride and the other astronauts soared into history.

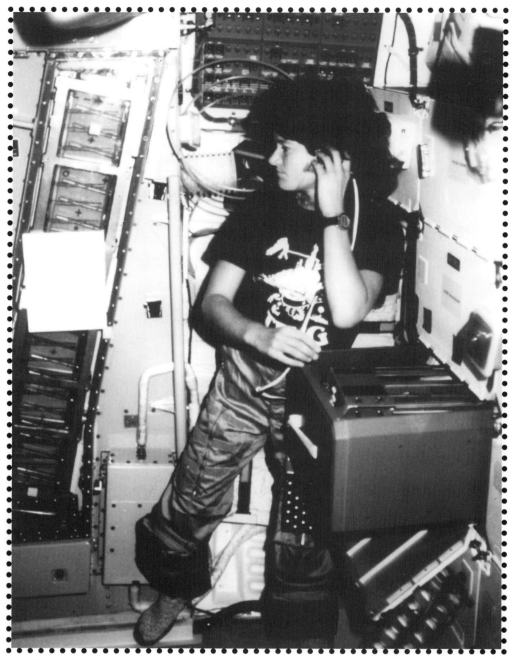

Sally communicates with ground control from the mid deck of the Space Shuttle Challenger. She has just opened one of the large lockers for an experiment for NASA.

Chapter 5

Life Aboard the Challenger

• •

Once the shuttle was in orbit, the ride was quiet and peaceful. The engines shut down and only the hum of fans that circulated the air could be heard. The shuttle was flying so fast that it circled Earth every 90 minutes. The astronauts didn't feel like they were moving, but when they looked out the window they could see Earth passing quickly below.

Sally could not see the whole Earth at one time, but she described her view this way: "We still have a magnificent view. The sparkling blue oceans and bright orange deserts are glorious against the blackness of space. Even if we can't see the whole planet, we can see quite a distance. When we are over Los Angeles we can see as far as Oregon; when we are over Florida we can see New York.

"We see mountain ranges reaching up to us and canyons falling away. We see huge dust storms blowing over deserts in Africa and smoke spewing from the craters of active volcanoes in Hawaii. We see enormous chunks of ice floating in the Antarctic Ocean and electrical storms raging over the Atlantic."

Sally and the crew experienced 16 sunrises and 16 sunsets every 24 hours. When they slept they used black blinders so that the bright sunlight would not wake them.

Sally enjoyed the weightlessness. It seemed to be one big experiment and in each move she learned something new. She discovered that she had to push herself off from one of the walls if she wanted to cross the room. However, that push had to be gentle or she would bang into the other wall. The crew found that they could sit anyplace, even on the ceiling, so the working area in the cabin was not as confining as it had seemed. Since they could float from place to place in their cabin, they had to secure themselves when they slept.

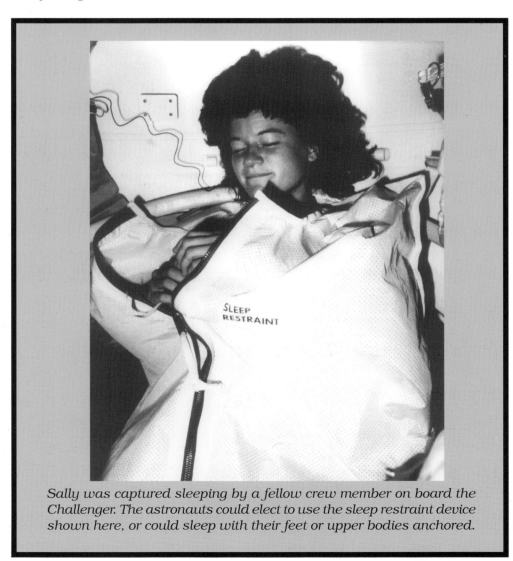

Sally was captured sleeping by a fellow crew member on board the Challenger. The astronauts could elect to use the sleep restraint device shown here, or could sleep with their feet or upper bodies anchored.

Eating was interesting. The crew took turns preparing meals. First they checked to see what food was scheduled. Then they secured a tray to their side with Velcro so that it wouldn't float away. Food came dehydrated in packages. An oven was in the spaceplane, so if the meal was to be hot, water was squeezed into the pack and then the pack was placed in the oven. The astronauts snipped open the pouches of food with scissors and ate it with spoons. The food was sticky, so it would stick to the spoon and not float away. If food escaped, it simply floated in the air. Sometimes the astronauts would play with their food.

Usually the crew members could all sleep at the same time because the computers were in charge. They might sleep head up or down. With no gravity, it really didn't matter. Sometimes they attached themselves to the wall, and sometimes they just slept and floated.

During the mission the astronauts could wear normal-looking clothes. They didn't have to wear helmets or face masks because the air was automatically controlled. Their clothes were loose and comfortable and had large pockets. In the pockets they put their spoons, scissors, tape recorders, tools, books, and nuts for snacking. When Sally dressed she could put on her pants both legs at a time.

There was a bathroom on the spaceplane but it was not like any ground-based bathroom. There was no sink because the water would simply have floated around in little blobs. When Sally washed her face each morning, she put her washcloth next to a water gun with a trigger control on the nozzle.

Sally used disposable toothbrushes that were preloaded with digestible toothpaste. After she brushed her

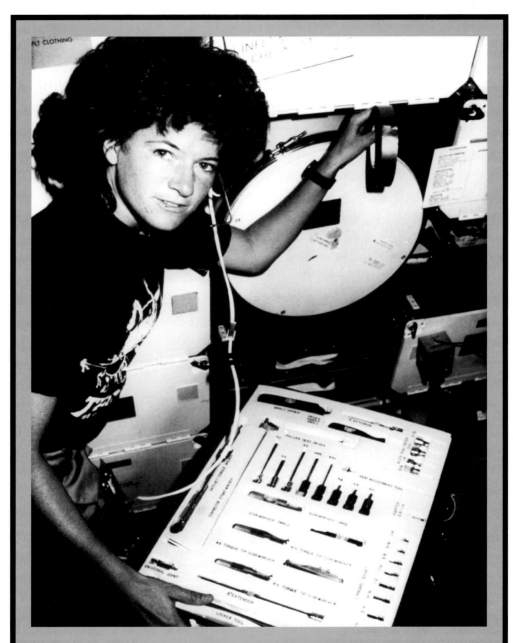

Sally displays an array of tools at her disposal on the mid deck of the Space Shuttle Challenger. The tools fit neatly inside a drawer located beneath the large drum-shaped object.

teeth she swallowed the toothpaste and threw the brush away.

The toilet in the spaceplane was built into one wall of the cabin. Each astronaut had a special cone-shaped cup that was held next to the body. It was important to turn on the air suction so that the urine would go down into the waste tank hidden beneath the floor. Other times, the astronaut would sit on the seat and use leg restraints to stay seated. Again the air suction would be turned on to replace gravity, and the waste would be pulled down into the tank.

Housekeeping was done every day and was very important. Little vacuums were used to polish computer terminals and clean the air of dust, hair and crumbs. Any spills had to be caught right away. Can you imagine bumping into a glob of orange juice or coffee?

Getting into orbit was just one step to the mission. While the astronauts certainly enjoyed the thrill of liftoff, each one had some big jobs to accomplish. There were satellites to launch and experiments to do over the next six days. As soon as the space shuttle was in orbit, Sally Ride and the crew of *Challenger* went to work.

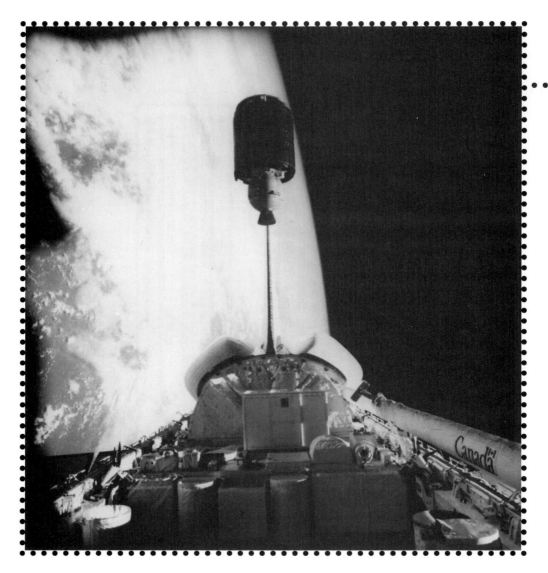

The remote manipulator arm is used to place the Indonesian Palapa B communications satellite in orbit. This was one of the jobs for the STS-7 crew.

Chapter 6
Sally at Work

A fter all the excitement of the launch, the STS-7 crew began to do all the jobs that were assigned. The first task was to launch the ANIK-C Canadian communications satellite. The purpose of the satellite was to relay voice, pictures, and information throughout Canada. One of the ways that NASA pays for the costs of exploring space is to launch satellites for large corporations or for other countries.

With orbits only taking 90 minutes, the seventh orbit began at about 10 hours and 30 minutes after liftoff. During that time Sally and John Fabian were getting ready. They took their places at the control panel located at the rear of the flight deck. Windows let them see the cargo bay where the satellite was stored.

The first step was to open the sun shield that protected the satellite from heat during the flight. Once the sun shield was opened, the 7,400-pound satellite popped into position. It began to spin on a turntable. Then *Challenger*'s computer commanded the strong clamps holding the satellite to release it into space.

The satellite had its own small rocket booster. Forty-five minutes later, when *Challenger* was a safe distance away, the rocket fired and sent the satellite on its way to orbit over 22,000 miles above Earth.

With the ANIK-C on its way, Sally's first day in space came to an end. Each move had been a success. The astronauts spent their first night in space resting easy.

On the second day in space the crew launched Palapa B, a satellite from the Republic of Indonesia. Norm Thagard measured everyone's heart rates and breathing patterns during this operation as one of the experiments. Indonesia, which is located in the Indian Ocean, is made up of 13,677 islands. The satellite would make it easier for people on different islands to communicate with each other.

To launch these satellites everything had to be just right. There was an exact place above Earth from which they had to be released, and the shuttle had to be pointing in exactly the right direction. Two astronauts sat with seat belts in place at the computers; another was near the windows; and a fourth was floating behind the seats near the satellite switches. The countdown was the same—*ten, nine, eight . . .* —as for the shuttle launch.

There was also free time each day. A treadmill was anchored to the shuttle so that the astronauts could exercise. They had to tether themselves to it. After running, Sally noted that she was "probably one of the few people to run across the Indian Ocean."

Days three and four were filled with doing scientific experiments. There was a colony of carpenter ants on board. This experiment looked at how microgravity affects the social structure of an ant society. Another experiment was to see how sunflower and radish seedlings respond to weightlessness. Its purpose was to teach future space farmers how to get roots to grow down and stalks to grow up without gravity.

During this time they also did experiments trying to find ways of making new substances such as medicines, metals and crystals in weightlessness.

To help scientists understand the effects of weightlessness on the human body, the astronauts recorded data about their own bodies. This data would help future astronauts on longer trips.

On the fifth day of the mission, Sally Ride and John Fabian used the remote manipulator system to launch a two-ton West German Shuttle Pallet Satellite (SPAS). It looked like a flat cart, or pallet, piled high with packages. The packages contained eleven experiments.

Sally and John took their places at the control panel. Sally called out the commands while John pushed buttons on the panel to lift the SPAS out of the cargo bay. When it was out of the bay, they let it drift alongside the shuttle. Both vehicles were speeding at 17,000 miles per hour. Two hours later, Bob Crippen moved the orbiter closer to the SPAS, and John caught it again with the robot arm.

John and Sally changed places. Sally now used the arm and John called out the commands. The idea was to release and retrieve the satellite without using too much of the shuttle's fuel. This practice of catching and releasing the SPAS was a rehearsal for the day when the shuttle would retrieve crippled satellites and park them in the cargo bay for repairs.

Then Bob fired a small engine on *Challenger* to move it away from the SPAS. A camera mounted on the satellite took photographs of the shuttle. They were the first photographs taken of the shuttle while it was flying in space.

All together, the astronauts released the satellite and retrieved it five times. Then the satellite was stowed in the cargo bay. The whole operation took more than nine hours.

NASA scientists were proud of the astronauts. They had completed their experiments successfully.

On Thursday, the sixth day, the crew began stowing all the equipment in preparation for their return home. It had been a successful flight in every way.

They had planned to be the first to land at the new three-mile strip at Kennedy Space Center. However, the weather did not cooperate. There were low clouds and light rain in the area. This moisture in the Florida air could damage *Challenger*'s fragile insulating tiles. NASA decided it would be best to land the shuttle at Edwards Air Force Base in California's Mojave Desert.

Many people were disappointed, including Sally's parents. They were waiting for her in Florida.

The landing was flawless. Commander Robert Crippen fired twin-braking rockets on orbit 97, above the Indian Ocean, to start *Challenger*'s hour-long descent toward a dead-stick landing on the dry lakebed at Edwards. At 78,000 feet, Crippen switched from automatic pilot and assumed manual control for the wide sweeping turn that would bring it in line with the runway. He had just one chance to get it right: the shuttle operates like a glider during its descent, with no engines to power up for a second try.

The spacecraft was still moving at two hundred miles an hour when the rear wheels touched Runway 23 at Edwards AFB. Then the nosewheel came down and the crew of the *Challenger* was back on Earth. The mission had lasted 6 days, 2 hours, 23 minutes, 59 seconds. It had covered 2,530,567 miles during 97 orbits of the Earth at an altitude of 160 to 170 nautical miles.

Before the crew could leave the shuttle they had to practice walking and get used to gravity again. Everything seemed very heavy, even pencils. At first it was an effort for Sally to lift her hand.

The "sniffer crew," clad in white rubber suits and yellow booties, inspected the shuttle and determined that no dangerous fumes were leaking from the *Challenger.*

Then the astronauts emerged, led by Commander Crippen. His crew followed: pilot Frederick Hauck, mission specialists Sally Ride and John Fabian, and finally Norman Thagard.

About 125 people had quickly gathered to welcome the astronauts, and they cheered for the happy crew. They knew the experiments from this trip into space would help many astronauts in the future. It had indeed been a great success.

At a press conference following the landing, Sally Ride said, "The thing that I'll remember most about the flight is that it was fun. In fact, I'm sure it was the most fun that I will ever have in my life."

But Sally was to have that fun once more.

Commander Robert Crippen brings the Orbiter Challenger to touchdown on Edwards runway 23, at the conclusion of STS-7. The flight was scheduled to land at Kennedy Space Center, until NASA officials diverted it to Edwards Air Force Base. Fog at the Cape reduced visibility.

Chapter 7

Sally Goes Up Again

• •

S ally Ride was constantly sought after for interviews and endorsements. She refused all invitations that did not include her fellow crew members. She always said that they were a team and her being a woman did not justify any special attention.

Following three weeks of debriefings, Sally was given a new assignment. She was to act as a liaison officer between NASA and private defense contractors and aerospace companies seeking to purchase space aboard the shuttle.

Before long, NASA chose Sally Ride to be in a *Challenger* crew again. It would be on STS 41-G, the thirteenth space shuttle flight. Captain Robert Crippen would also command this flight. The crew members were Jon A. McBride, pilot; Sally K. Ride, Kathryn D. Sullivan and David C. Leestma, mission specialists; Marc Garneau and Paul D. Scully-Power, payload specialists.

On October 5, 1984, at 7:03 A.M. EDT, the launch of 41-G lifted off as scheduled. It was a very busy eight-day mission and the crew went to work right away. They deployed the Earth Radiation Budget Satellite (ERBS) less than nine hours into the flight. The Office of Space and Terrestrial Applications-3 (OSTA-3) carried three experiments in the payload bay. They studied Earth from space using special radar equipment and cameras and made demonstrations by the Orbital Refueling System (ORS) to show that it is possible to refuel satellites in orbit.

The crew of mission 41-G: bottom, l to r: Jon McBride, Sally Ride, Kathryn Sullivan, David Leestma. Top: Paul Scully-Power, Robert Crippen, and Marc Garneau.

Each day presented new challenges, and the crew had to make changes along the way. On the first day Sally was to deploy a satellite that would help scientists make better long-range weather forecasts. The satellite had two solar panels that had been folded in the cargo bay. In space, they would not open because the hinges had frozen.

This was a problem that Sally had never encountered in the flight simulators. After several tries, she finally turned the satellite so that the hinges would thaw in the sunlight. The panels opened and she was able to ease the satellite out of the cargo bay and on its way.

The next day Ride had to use the RMS to reach into the cargo bay and close a panel. Her training and ability to make these corrections helped to make this a successful flight.

This was the first flight to include two women. Kathryn Sullivan became the first woman to walk in space.

The mission ended on October 13, 1984, at 12:26 P.M. on Runway 33 of Kennedy Space Center. It had lasted 8 days, 5 hours, 23 minutes, 33 seconds and flew a distance of 3,289,444 miles at an altitude of 218 nautical miles.

Sally worked every day conducting simulated tests, preparing for her space flights, or testing conditions for other astronauts.

On March 15, 2000, Sally christened the Goodyear Blimp. She took an inaugural ride with pilot Don McDuff.

Chapter 8
After NASA

● ●

In June 1985, Sally Ride was assigned to a third space shuttle flight. Training for the flight was interrupted on January 28, 1986, by the space shuttle *Challenger* accident. The shuttle exploded only a few seconds after liftoff, killing all seven crew members. Within days of the disaster, President Ronald Reagan selected Sally Ride to serve with 12 others as a member of the Presidential Commission investigating the accident.

The reason for the accident was found quickly. A seal at the aft end of one of the solid rocket boosters had failed. It consisted of a metal interconnection with two O-rings in the leakage path. O-rings look like slender rubber doughnuts and are in round grooves that contain a pressurized fluid. The fluid, in attempting to escape, deforms the O-ring to better seal the joint. Since O-rings are resilient, they can make up for small motions and small irregularities in the joint.

Unfortunately, the critical resilience of O-rings depends on their temperature, and the launch was on an unusually cold day. Ice was found on the launchpad that morning, and the air temperature was 36 degrees at the time of launch, 15 degrees cooler than any other launch. This temperature dependence had been a concern of engineers during the development of the booster and had been communicated to company managers and NASA officials. In fact, an engineer had attempted to have the *Challenger* launch delayed that day because of this low temperature but had been unsuccessful.

Analysis of photographs verified the reason for the explosion. Dark puffs of smoke were seen just seconds after launch. That indicated burning grease and O-ring material. Then the smoke color changed abruptly, indicating that the main tank had ruptured, adding hydrogen to the flame. Approximately 72 seconds after launch, the rear strut linking the solid rocket booster to the shuttle parted, permitting the booster to pivot around the forward strut. Then the dome of the liquid-hydrogen tank dropped away, releasing the load of hydrogen and creating a thrust of some 2.8 million pounds that shoved the remainder of the tank toward the oxygen tank. At about the same time, the pivoting solid booster hit the bottom of the oxygen tank. The explosion immediately followed. The villain was obviously a joint design that was inadequate for the environment.

The commission dealt with the following question: Was the design faulty or was the launch environment too risky?

Their findings demanded an improved seal design. They called for a safety audit of other critical shuttle subsystems, a provision for crew escape in the case of launch abort, and improvements in the landing characteristics.

This report, called the Rogers Commission Report, changed many things in NASA. President Reagan ordered NASA to change its priorities. The primary purpose would no longer be to launch satellites. Changes needed to be made not only in the routine safety of the shuttles themselves, but also in how decisions were made at NASA. The Rogers Commission suggested that astronauts with years of experience in space should be involved in management decisions.

Sally Ride was reassigned to NASA headquarters in Washington, D.C. She became the first working astronaut to cross the line into administration. New goals were to be set.

Some wanted to return to the moon. Others, especially scientists interested in space, wanted to send astronauts to Mars. Sally said that we must be concerned with not just going into space but what we were going to do when we got there.

During this time Sally wrote a report on leadership at NASA titled *Leadership and America's Future in Space.* Her main goal was to get NASA back on track. She suggested that NASA focus on four major areas: (1) Mission to Planet Earth: a program that would use the perspective afforded from space to study and characterize our home planet on a global scale; (2) Exploration of the Solar System: a program to retain U.S. leadership in exploration of the outer solar system and to regain U.S. leadership in exploration of comets, asteroids, and Mars; (3) Outpost on the Moon: a program that would build on and extend the legacy of the Apollo program; (4) Humans to Mars: a program to send astronauts on a series of round-trips to land on the surface of Mars, leading to the eventual establishment of a permanent base there.

In 1987 Sally Ride left NASA to accept a fellowship at the Stanford University Center for International Security and Arms Control. This was also the year she was divorced from Steven Hawley.

Ride has written several books for children. She coauthored a book with Susan Okie called *To Space & Back,* which describes her experiences in space. She has also coauthored three books with Tam O'Shaughnessy: *Voyager: An Adventure to the Edge of the Solar System* in 1992, *The Third Planet: Exploring the Earth from Space* in 1994, and *The Mystery of Mars* in 1999. She received the Jefferson Award for Public Service and the National Spaceflight Medal and she is a member of the President's Committee of Advisors on Science and Technology.

Since 1989, Dr. Ride has been on the faculty of the University of California at San Diego. There she is a physics professor. As a physicist, she could now follow her own research interests, the theory of free electron lasers. Her research has contributed to the general knowledge of how lasers work. As others also work with lasers, new uses have been found, especially in the medical field. Lasers are being used more and more in surgery because they reduce risk to the patient and shorten the time a patient is hospitalized. Ride has been a part of these discoveries that have advanced technology.

She was also the director of the California Space Institute, a research institute of the University of California, San Diego. There she was in charge of space-related activities.

In 2001 she founded Imaginary Lines, a group that supports girls who are or who might become interested in science, math or technology. The organization wants to "increase the number of girls who are technically literate and who have the foundation they need to go on in science, math, or engineering." Ride says that in the fourth grade the number of girls and boys who like math and science is about the same. However, by the eighth grade twice as many boys as girls show an interest in these subjects. She wants to keep math and science interesting for girls so that they will continue studying these subjects and get more involved in science careers.

Ride says, "One of our goals is to make girls feel like they belong to the scientific community and help them connect to this community and stay involved."

Sally Ride Science Clubs are forming all over the country, enabling girls to consult with experts, exchange ideas, collaborate with peers and embark on all sorts of online and offline adventures. Club members can contribute stories to a national newsletter, learn how cell phones work, design tech toys, invent devices to help astronauts live in weightlessness and attend science festivals.

Today, Sally Ride still enjoys flying a Grumman Tiger aircraft. She speaks at scientific conventions around the world. Although she left the California Space Institute as director in 1996, she continues to teach in the physics department at the University of California, San Diego. She is still an inspiring scientist.

Dr. Sally Ride, the first woman in space, left a stamp on the space program that few astronauts, male or female, have been able to equal. Her contributions have not only been notable in NASA but also to the students she works with today.

Sally Ride has certainly unlocked many scientific secrets both in space and on Earth. She is indeed a role model and a challenger.

Sally Ride Chronology

1951 born May 26 in Encino, California

1968 graduates from Westlake School for Girls in Los Angeles

1968 attends Swarthmore College in Swarthmore, Pennsylvania

1973 earns two degrees from Stanford University: a B.S. in physics and a B.A. in English

1975 receives a master's degree in physics from Stanford University

1978 earns a Ph.D. in astrophysics from Stanford University; enters NASA astronaut training

1982 marries astronaut Steven Hawley

1983 first U.S. woman in space on STS-7, June 18–24

1984 second shuttle mission on STS 41-G, October 5–13

1985 assigned to third shuttle flight; assigned to presidential panel to investigate the *Challenger* disaster; assigned to NASA headquarters in Washington, D.C.; *Leadership and America's Future in Space* is published

1986 *To Space & Back* is published

1987 leaves NASA to take a two-year appointment at Stanford University; divorces Steven Hawley

1989 becomes professor of physics at the University of California, San Diego; becomes part-time director of the California Space Institute

1992 *Voyager: An Adventure to the Edge of the Solar System* is published

1994 *The Third Planet: Exploring the Earth from Space* is published

1996 leaves California Space Institute as director

1999 *The Mystery of Mars* is published

2001 founds Imaginary Lines

Spaceflight Timeline

1926 Robert H. Goddard fires first liquid propellant rocket.

1957 USSR launches *Sputnik 1*, first Earth satellite (October 4), then *Sputnik 2*, which carries the dog Laika (November 3).

1958 First U.S. satellite, *Explorer 1*, is launched (January 31); NASA is created (October).

1961 USSR sends Yuri Gagarin into Earth orbit on *Vostok 1* (April 12); American Alan B. Shepard makes suborbital flight on Mercury *Freedom 7* (May 5).

1961–1963 USSR sends up five more piloted Vostok craft, including *Vostok 6*, piloted by first woman in space, Valentina V. Tereskova (June 16, 1963); U.S. sends up six more piloted Mercury craft.

1964 USSR launches *Voskhod 1*, the first three-man spacecraft.

1965–1966 U.S. launches Gemini spacecraft: *Gemini 3* carries Virgil Grissom; the others carry two men each. *Gemini 4* carries James McDivitt and Edward White; White makes the first U.S. space walk (June 3, 1965).

1969 Neil A. Armstrong, Edwin E. Aldrin, Jr., and Michael Collins fly *Apollo 11* to the moon; Armstrong and Aldrin make first moon walk (July 20).

1973 *Skylab 1*, first U.S. space station, is placed in orbit (May 14).

1975 U.S. and USSR cooperate on first international space mission, docking an American Apollo craft with a Soviet Soyuz craft (July 17).

1977 U.S. space shuttle makes its first test flight on top of a Boeing 747 (February 18).

1981 John Young and Robert Crippen take U.S. space shuttle *Columbia* on its first orbital test flight (April 12–14).

1983 Paul Weitz, Karol Bobko, Story Musgrave, and Donald Peterson take the space shuttle *Challenger* on its first orbital flight (April 4–9); Sally Ride becomes the first American woman in space, flying aboard the *Challenger* on STS-7 (June 18).

1986 Space Shuttle *Challenger* explodes shortly after liftoff (January 28) killing all on board, including school teacher Christa McAuliffe. The explosion causes 2 1/2-year delay in further Shuttle launches while investigations and redesign take place.

1988 First launch of *Discovery* with redesigned O-rings in the solid boosters.

2000 Astronaut Bill Shepherd launched to live in the International Space Station.

2002 International Space Station visible to the United States just before dawn the first week in September

2006 Planned completion of the International Space Station, which will be about the size of a 3-bedroom home and will house up to 7 astronauts working on numerous scientific experiments.

Further Reading

Books

Blacknall, Carolyn. *Sally Ride: America's First Woman in Space.* New York: Dillon Press, 1984.

Camp, Carole Ann. *Sally Ride: First American Woman in Space.* Springfield, N.J.: Enslow Publishers, Inc., 1997.

Kramer, Barbara. *Sally Ride: A Space Biography.* Springfield, N.J.: Enslow Publishers, Inc., 1998.

Launius, Roger D., and Bertram Ulrich. *NASA & The Exploration of Space.* New York: Stewart, Tabori & Chang, 1998.

Ride, Sally, and Susan Okie. *To Space & Back.* New York: Lothrop, Lee & Shepard Books, 1986.

Ride, Sally, and Tam O'Shaughnessy. *The Mystery of Mars.* New York: Crown Publishers, Inc., 1999.

———. *The Third Planet: Exploring the Earth from Space.* New York: Crown Publishers, Inc., 1994.

———. *Voyager: An Adventure to The Edge of the Solar System.* New York: Crown Publishers, Inc., 1992.

Wallace, Lane E. *Flights of Discovery: 50 Years at the NASA Dryden Flight Research Center.* Washington, D.C.: NASA History Office, 1996.

Internet Addresses

http://www.bena.com/lucidcafe/library/96may/ride.html

http://calspace.ucsd.edu

http://earth.jsc.nasa.gov

http://imaginarylinesinc.com

http://www.jsc.nasa.gov

http://www.jsc.nasa.gov/er/seh/ride.htm

http://www.nasajobs.nasa.gov

http://www.sallyrideclub.com

http://www.space.com

http://spaceflight.NASA.gov/shuttle/future/2002overview.html

http://spacelink.msfc.nasa.gov

Glossary of Terms

ANIK-C—a Canadian communications satellite named from the Inuit language meaning "brother."

astronaut—a person who pilots a spacecraft or works in space, particularly in the space program of the United States. It comes from the Greek words meaning "space sailor."

astrophysics—the study of energy between planets and stars.

capcom—*cap*sule *com*municator, the person who relays information between Mission Control and the astronauts during a flight.

dead-stick landing—a landing made without power.

debriefing—to answer and share information upon return from a mission.

g force—the pressure one feels with great acceleration. One g equals the force of gravity on Earth on a body at rest.

laser—a very powerful and focused light source.

mission specialists—scientists who do experiments on spaceflights.

NASA—National Aeronautics and Space Administration, the U.S. government group that explores space.

payload—the experiments that will be given top priority during a space mission.

RMS—Remote Manipulator System, a 50-foot-long robotic arm used to move cargo in and out of the shuttle's cargo bay.

resilient—able to bounce back into shape after being deformed or stressed.

satellite—a spacecraft that is sent into orbit around Earth, the moon, or another heavenly body.

shuttle—a reusable spacecraft in which the astronauts stay during a mission. It is often called a spaceplane.

simulator—a computer-driven vehicle in which a person can sit and experience a spaceflight. It is used by astronauts to help them prepare for emergencies in space.

SPAS—Shuttle Pallet Satellite.

STS—Space Transportation System, a reusable spacecraft.

white room—the room in which the astronauts prepare to enter the space shuttle. It is dust-free and cleaner than an operating room.

Index